Very Best (almost) Friends

Poems of Friendship

collected by
Paul B. Janeczko

illustrated by
Christine Davenier

CANDLEWICK PRESS
CAMBRIDGE, MASSACHUSETTS

Contents

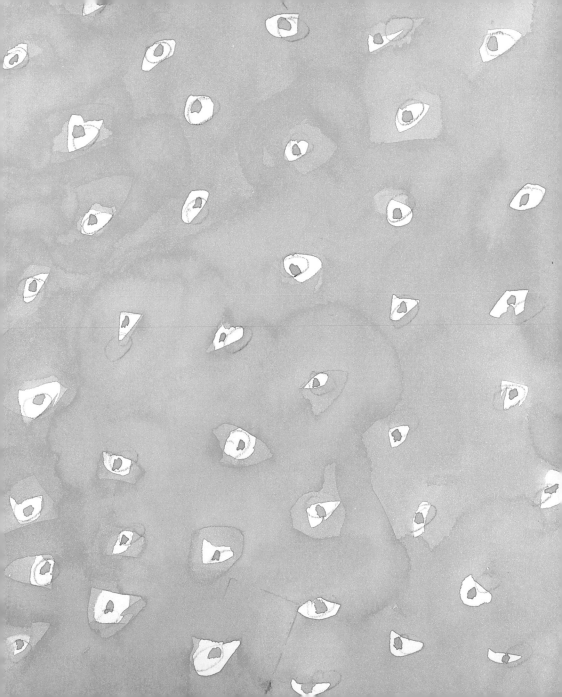

First edition 1999

Library of Congress Cataloging-in-Publication Data is available.

Library of Congress Catalog Card Number 98-10782

ISBN 0-7636-0475-5

10 9 8 7 6 5 4 3 2

Printed in Hong Kong/China

This book was typeset in Colwell.
The pictures were done in watercolor and pen and ink.

Candlewick Press
2067 Massachusetts Avenue
Cambridge, Massachusetts 02140

For Jerry Weiss —
friend, mentor, godfather —
another good guy from New Jersey
P. B. J.

For my friend Edmund White
C. D.

Friendship

There is a secret thread that makes us friends
 Turn away from hard and breakful eyes
 Turn away from cold and painful lies
That speaks of other, more important ends
There are two hard yet tender hearts that beat
 Take always my hand at special times
 Take always my dark and precious rhymes
That sing so brightly when our glad souls meet

WALTER DEAN MYERS

9

Finding a Way

I'd like you for a friend.
I'd like to find the way
Of asking you to be my friend.
I don't know what to say.

What would you like to hear?
What is it I can do?
There has to be some word, some look
Connecting me to you.

MYRA COHN LIVINGSTON

Lonesome

Lonesome all alone
Listens for the phone.

Listens for a call,
Anyone at all.

Listens for a ring,
Saying anything.

Lonesome all alone
Listens for the phone.

Myra Cohn Livingston

11

The Dollar Dog

I had a dollar dog named Spot.
He wasn't much, but he was a lot
Of *kinds* of dog, plus a few parts flea,
Seven parts yapper, and seventy-three
Or seventy-four parts this-and-that.
The only thing he wasn't was cat.
He was collie-terrier-spaniel-hound
And everything else they have at the pound.
Yes, some might call him a mongrel, but
To me he was thoroughbred, pedigreed mutt.
A middle-sized nothing, or slightly smaller,
But a lot of kinds to get for a dollar.

JOHN CIARDI

Jim

There never was a nicer boy
Than Mrs. Jackson's Jim.
The sun should drop its greatest gold
On him.

Because, when Mother-dear was sick,
He brought her cocoa in.
And brought her broth, and brought her bread.
And brought her medicine.

And, tipping, tidied up her room.
And would not let her see
He missed his game of baseball
Terribly.

GWENDOLYN BROOKS

13

My Stupid Parakeet Named After You
(from a letter to a best friend)

You know my stupid parakeet
Named after you? (He has big feet.)
Well, he cracked his beak. Ran into a lamp.
The vet applied a little clamp.

But that's not all. Whenever he naps,
He falls right off his perch and flaps
So hard he almost flies apart.
Compared to that dumb bird, you're smart.

X. J. KENNEDY

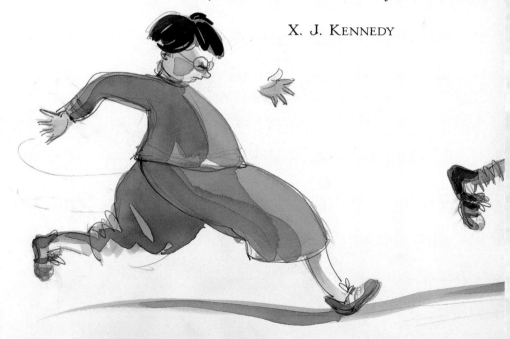

And Some More Wicked Thoughts

In every race I've ever run
I'm number two; Joe's number one.
There's awful things that I could do
To make me one and make Joe two.
(But I won't even think of them.)

JUDITH VIORST

Gang

Like a rushing wind
        the street gang came
Around the corner
        as if playing a game.
Threw stones in windows,
        spilled every trash can,
While onlookers stared,
        then, frightened, ran.

Came the police
        out of nowhere, quick,
All in uniform,
        each with his stick;
The gang disappeared
        like a sudden shower,
The street stayed empty
        for many an hour.

LOIS LENSKI

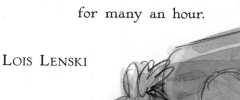

17

Toby Twits Tina

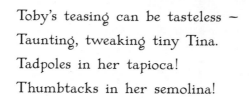

Toby's teasing can be tasteless —
Taunting, tweaking tiny Tina.
Tadpoles in her tapioca!
Thumbtacks in her semolina!

Toby ought to be more tactful.
If he's tempted to torment her,
Let him tickle, *never* throttle,
Never thump her, lest he dent her.

JEANNE STEIG

Teased

Sometimes
when I'm teased
I don't cry,
I go away.
When I come back
my brother and his friends
are doing something else.
I remember.
They forget.

RICHARD J. MARGOLIS

Summertime Sharing

Danitra sits hunched on the stoop and pouts.
I ask her what there is to pout about.
"Nothin' much," she says to me,
but then I see her eyes following the ice cream man.

I shove my hand into my pocket
and find the change there where I left it.
"Be right back," I yell, running down the street.
Me and my fast feet are there and back in just two shakes.

Danitra breaks the Popsicle in two and gives me half.
The purple ice trickles down her chin. I start to laugh.
Her teeth flash in one humongous grin,
telling me she's glad that I'm her friend without even saying a word.

NIKKI GRIMES

People

Some people talk and talk
and never say a thing.
Some people look at you
and birds begin to sing.

Some people laugh and laugh
and yet you want to cry.
Some people touch your hand
and music fills the sky.

CHARLOTTE ZOLOTOW

Blubber Lips

"Blubber Lips, Blubber Lips,
here comes Blubber Lips,"
we taunted Blubber Lips home
from school each day.
His lips like pillows of flesh
stuck out from the unmade bed of his face.
We danced around him, sang our song
as he steady walked silent.
"Blubber Lips, Blubber Lips," every day,
until he punched me in the mouth
and gave me blubber lips
and I learned his real name.

JIM DANIELS

Another Poem to Send to Your Worst Enemy

Dweeb, drip, softy, jerk,
Dope, sap, noodle, berk!
Fathead, bumpkin, duffer, mutt,
Loopy, potty, monkey nut!
Slimy crawler, teacher's pet.
Flat-foot-duck-toed-knock-kneed sweat!
Fleabag, snot-rag, waxy-ears.
Hope your acne never clears!
Airhead, doughbrain, pizzaface.
Reject from the human race!
Spotty stinkpot, silly fool.
Donkey, pinhead, pimply mule!
Blockhead, bonkers, soppy, wet —
Just how stupid can you get?

COLIN McNAUGHTON

Peter the Pain

Peter is sitting
Beside me again,
Says I have mush
Instead of a brain,

Steals my pencil
And gives it to Wayne,
Gets me in trouble
With Mrs. McShane.

Move me to China,
To France or to Spain.
Just get me away from

Peter the Pain!

KALLI DAKOS

If I Could Put a Curse on You

If I could put a curse on you
I would have a laugh or two

    May your gym shorts drop below your knees
    May your locker fill with killer bees

    May you bust the spokes on your new bike
    May your girlfriend tell you, "Take a hike!"

    May you muff the science on the test
    May you skulk around the halls half dressed

    May your parents find out what you did
    May the bully find out where you hid

    May your lunch get swiped and eaten
    May all your favorite teams get beaten

    May you get a pimple on your nose
    May you grow an extra pair of toes

Oh, if I could put a curse on you
I would have a laugh or two!

PAUL B. JANECZKO

The Marmalade Man
Makes a Dance to Mend Us

Tiger, Sunflowers, King of Cats,
Cow and Rabbit, mend your ways.
I the needle, you the thread —
follow me through mist and maze.

Fox and hound, go paw in paw.
Cat and rat, be best of friends.
Lamb and tiger, walk together.
Dancing starts where fighting ends.

NANCY WILLARD

Friends

I fear it's very wrong of me
And yet I must admit,
When someone offers friendship
I want the *whole* of it.
I don't want everybody else
To share my friends with me.
At least, I want *one* special one,
Who, indisputably,

Likes me much more than all the rest,
Who's always on my side,
Who never cares what others say,
Who lets me come and hide
Within his shadow, in his house –
It doesn't matter where –
Who lets me simply be myself,
Who's always, *always* there.

ELIZABETH JENNINGS

Who?

Who is my very best almost friend?
I'll start by saying, "Not you."

The End

JOHN CIARDI

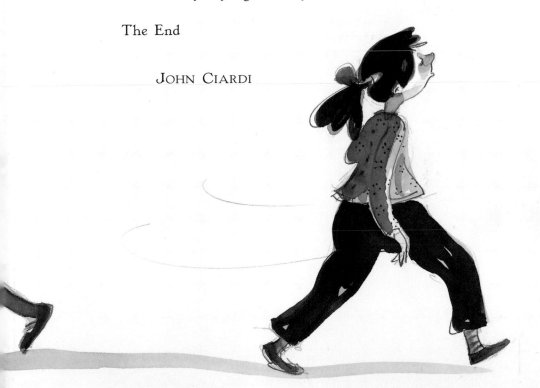

Friends

I am drawing a picture
My house is in it
A jagged yellow sun
hangs from the blue strip
of sky   I am drawing
a dog   His tail is wagging
He wants to be
my dog

I am drawing
the sound of a train far off
I will   scribble in
some smoke   I might want to
travel

Your house is in my picture
It is leaning across our street
I am putting the word POW!
and electric zigzags
where our chimneys
almost touch

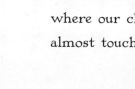

In this picture
I am waving from my window   You
are running up our walk
A bird is flying off the edge
of the page   singing
Anything can happen
in pictures

I don't
need to draw our faces
We will never forget
each other

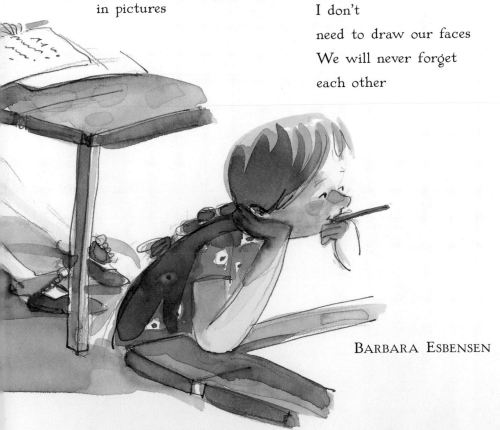

Barbara Esbensen

31

A Trade

I'll trade you my kingdom for your song
I'll trade you my song for your colour
I'll trade you my colour for your story
I'll trade you my story for your dance
I'll trade you my dance for your daydream
I'll trade you my daydream for your hand
I'll trade you my hand for your hand

ZARO WEIL

I Still Have Everything You Gave Me

It is dusty on the edges.

It is slightly rotten.

I guard it without thinking.

I focus on it once a year
when I shake it out in the wind.

I do not ache.

I would not trade.

NAOMI SHIHAB NYE

Listening

My friend has a voice
wild with roses and thorn.
I've hidden in thickets
of her song, surrounded
by their scent, sight, sting.

BETSY HEARNE

34

To You

I think I could walk
through the simmering sand
if I held your hand.
I think I could swim
the skin shivering sea
if you would accompany me.
And run on ragged, windy heights,
climb rugged rocks
and walk on air.

I think I could do anything at all,
if you were there.

KARLA KUSKIN

Permissions

37